D0205854

SUPER DC HEROES

SUPERMAN

THE MUSEUM MONSTERS

WRITTEN BY
MICHAEL DAHL

ILLUSTRATED BY
DAN SCHOENING

SUPERMAN CREATED BY
JERRY SIEGEL AND
JOE SHUSTER

STONE ARCH BOOKS
MINNEAPOLIS   SAN DIEGO

Published by Stone Arch Books in 2009
151 Good Counsel Drive, P.O. Box 669
Mankato, Minnesota 56002
www.stonearchbooks.com

Library of Congress Cataloging-in-Publication Data
Dahl, Michael.
    The Museum Monsters / by Michael Dahl; illustrated by Dan
Schoening.
    p. cm. — (DC Super Heroes. Superman)
    ISBN 978-1-4342-1157-6 (library binding)
    ISBN 978-1-4342-1372-3 (pbk.)
    [1. Superheroes—Fiction.] I. Schoening, Dan, ill. II. Title.
PZ7.D15134Mus 2009
[Fic]—dc22   2008032419

Summary: *Daily Planet* reporters Clark Kent and Lois Lane are covering
the opening of the new Metropolis Museum when, suddenly, a gigantic
skeleton of a blue whale comes to life. With lightning-speed, Superman
catches the colossal creature, but the magical mischief is far from over. The
impish Mr. Mxyzptlk has returned from the Fifth Dimension with dozens
troublesome tricks. Even the Man of Steel is helpless against the power of
magic!

Art Director: Bob Lentz
Designer: Brann Garvey

1 2 3 4 5 6 14 13 12 11 10 09

TABLE OF CONTENTS

CHAPTER 1

THE WORLD'S BIGGEST SKELETON

A flood of people swarmed outside the Metropolitan Museum of Natural History. They pushed against the glass and metal doors. They crowded the wide stone steps.

It was opening day. A new exhibit was on display: Monsters of the Deep. In half an hour the museum doors would open and thousands of visitors would rush inside.

At the back of the museum was a smaller door. It faced a quiet alley. There were no crowds back here. The museum director opened the door and peeked out.

"Quick!" he said. "Come in before anyone sees you!"

Two visitors followed him in. They were reporters for the *Daily Planet* newspaper, Lois Lane and Clark Kent. Lois threw her coat on a peg and rushed into the exhibit hall. Clark hurried up to follow her.

"Thanks for letting us in early," said Lois Lane. "This will give us a chance to see the new exhibit before the crowd pours in."

"You probably want to see the biggest display first," said the museum director.

"By the way, have you seen our friend, Jimmy Olsen?" Clark asked. "He's supposed to come and take photos for our story."

The director frowned. "Sorry," he said. "I'm the only one here. Except for our security guards at the front doors."

"That's funny," said Clark. "Jimmy's always on time."

"Don't worry about him," said Lois. "He'll show up soon."

Clark heard a strange buzzing sound. He glanced around but saw nothing. At first he thought it was a fly zipping past his ear.

"Our biggest exhibit is right through here," said the director. He led Lois and Clark through a tall stone hallway. They entered a giant room that soared five stories above the marble floor.

In the center of the room, hanging on metal wires high above their heads, was a huge skeleton.

"That's fantastic!" said Lois.

"It's the skeleton of a blue whale," explained the director. "The largest creature to ever live on the planet."

"Exactly how big is it?" asked Clark. He pulled out a small pad of paper and started jotting down notes.

The director stared up at the monster skeleton. "This one is over 110 feet long," he said. "When it was alive, it could hold over 90 tons of water in its mouth."

"Wow!" came a voice from nearby. "That whale's head is bigger than my whole apartment!"

"Jimmy!" said Lois.

At the other end of the large hall stood a redheaded teenager. He had a camera hanging from his neck and waved at the others. "Hi, Miss Lane. Hi, Mr. Kent."

"Jimmy," said Clark. "How did you get in here?"

"I have my ways," said Jimmy, smiling.

Clark heard the buzzing sound again. No one else in the room seemed to notice it, but that was not unusual. Clark Kent was actually Superman in disguise, the world's most powerful hero. And one of Superman's powers was super-hearing. He could hear sounds from miles away.

What was that buzzing, he wondered.

The sound seemed to be coming from another room. Clark looked up at a sign above the room's door. ENTOMOLOGY. Clark knew that meant insects. Maybe the buzzing had come from a bug, just as he thought.

As the others continued staring at the whale skeleton, Clark quickly stepped inside the insect room. The buzzing grew louder. Now it didn't sound like an insect at all. It sounded like a tiny voice. In fact, his super-hearing could pick up words. The voice was saying, "Superman! Help me!"

CHAPTER 2

THE WORLD'S SMALLEST REPORTER

Clark glanced around the insect room. All he saw were glass cases that held bugs from all over the world. The buzzing voice was coming from a case filled with leaves and branches. A sign on the case said:

WORLD'S SMALLEST REPORTER
Scientific Name: *J. Olsen*

Clark bent down to have a closer look. Inside the case sat a tiny, redheaded teenager waving and screaming.

"Help me, Mr. Kent!" the figure cried.

"Jimmy?" said Clark.

Quickly, Clark opened the lid of the case. He stuck in his hand and carefully picked up the tiny boy with his fingers. Then he set Jimmy on a nearby table. The boy stood no taller than the reporter's thumb.

"How did this happen?" asked Clark.

"I don't know," said Jimmy. "I was coming here to meet you and Miss Lane. The last thing I remember was knocking on the back door of the museum. Then I was inside that glass case. I could have ended up as bug food if you hadn't saved me."

Clark was confused. If this was the real Jimmy Olsen, who was the redheaded teenager in the other room? And who put the real Jimmy in the bug case?

Suddenly, a woman's scream echoed through the museum. AAAAHHHHHHHHHH!

"That's Lois," said Clark. "Will you be all right here, Jimmy?"

"No problem," said Jimmy. "I'll try to contact Superman with my signal-watch." Inside Jimmy's watch was a chip that could give off a supersonic beep. Only Superman's ears could hear the sound. "I hope it works at this size," added Jimmy.

"I think he's already here," said Clark.

"Really?" said Jimmy. While the teenager glanced around, searching for his superpowered friend, Clark raced out of the room. At the doorway to the whale exhibit, he froze. The blue whale's skeleton was moving. It swung back and forth.

At the other end of the room stood Lois and the museum director. Their eyes were glued to the moving skeleton.

"Watch out, Miss Lane!" warned the museum director.

TWANNNGG! One of the wires holding the skeleton snapped loose.

TWANNNGG! Another one broke.

Soon, the skeleton would crash to the floor. Clark dashed into a small nearby office. With super-speed he pulled off his reporter's clothes, revealing his Superman uniform underneath. Then he raced into the exhibit hall as the mighty Man of Steel.

"Superman!" yelled Lois.

He flew into the air. Another wire broke and the whale skeleton fell to the floor. Superman caught the skeleton easily in his arms. He gently set it on the shiny marble floor.

"Thank you, Superman!" the museum director cried. "That skeleton is priceless. If it had hit the floor, the bones would have shattered into a million pieces."

"Yes, thank you," added Lois.

Superman flew over to the reporter. "How did this happen?" he asked.

"I don't understand it," Lois said. "All of a sudden the skeleton began to shake."

Just then, the skeleton began to move its jaws. Its bony flippers waved up and down.

"It's alive!" said Lois.

"That's impossible!" said the museum director.

"It's very possible," said another voice. Superman turned to see Jimmy Olsen standing a few feet away.

The hero knew this was not the real Jimmy, but an imposter. The real teenage photographer was still shrunk to tiny size in the insect room.

"Who are you?" asked the Man of Steel.

The phony Jimmy Olsen laughed. His face changed shape. His red hair disappeared. He grew shorter. Then he began to spin around faster and faster.

Suddenly, floating a few yards from Superman's face was a weird little man wearing a purple hat. "Who in the world is that?" asked Lois.

"That's just the problem," said Superman. "He's not from this world. It's Mr. Mxyzptlk from the Fifth Dimension!"

CHAPTER 3

THE MISCHIEF MAKER

"Mr. what?" asked Lois.

The odd little imp took off his hat and bowed. "Just call me Mxy," he said. "Only Super Duper Man has ever been able to pronounce my real name."

"What are you doing here?" demanded Superman.

"You don't sound very happy to see me," said Mr. Mxyzptlk, frowning. "I came here to help you celebrate."

"Celebrate?" asked Superman.

"The opening of this amazing museum," said the strange imp. "Nobody knows how to have a fun time like me, right, buddy?"

The museum director was confused and annoyed. "You mean, it was you who caused those wires to break?" he yelled. "Do you have any idea of the damage you could have caused? These objects are priceless."

"You need to relax," said Mxy, pointing at the man. "Too much worrying can turn you into a bag of bones."

The museum director was changed into a living skeleton. His clothes hung on a frame of bones. His bony feet slipped out of his shoes. He was unable to speak because his tongue was gone.

"Turn him back," Superman ordered.

Mr. Mxyzptlk ignored the super hero and flew toward the ceiling. "Let's have a party!" shouted the mischievous imp. He clapped his hands together.

"Now what's happening?" asked Lois.

A glittering whirlwind filled the room. Tiny lights of different colors sparkled and whirled around her and Superman. Soon, the lights grew larger and thicker. They looked like floating crystal bowls.

"Look out, Lois!" said Superman. "Those are flying jellyfish."

Hundreds of jellyfish swam through the air. Below their shining heads hung long spindly arms. These arms, or tentacles, each carried a poisonous stinger at the end. One stab of poison could kill a human.

Superman was not human. He was a visitor from the planet Krypton, which was light-years away from Earth. The Earth's yellow sun had given his alien body powers far beyond those of mortal men. But even he was helpless against the forces of Mr. Mxyzptlk's magic. The stingers of these nightmare jellyfish might be able to stab even Superman's unbreakable skin.

"Don't you like my little friends?" said Mxy. "They're here to help us celebrate the wonderful world of sea creatures."

"Get behind me, Lois," said Superman.

The reporter ducked behind the man's massive shoulders. Then the super hero took in a deep breath. With the power of his superpowered lungs, he blew out a powerful wind. The wind shoved the jellyfish away from him and Lois.

"That's a great idea," said Mr. Mxyzptlk with a laugh. "I always thought you were a blowhard. Now, you can be — a blowfish!"

Superman's body began to expand like a balloon. He stared in horror as his arms grew flat and flabby and then turned into flippers. His mouth grew wide. His uniform was covered with orange, prickly scales. Long spikes stuck out from his back, his sides, and his stomach.

The weird fish hung in the center of the room. Its huge eyes stared in anger at the little imp. Meanwhile, Mxy was doubled over in laughter.

Lois Lane was so angry that tears came to her eyes. "You can't do that to Superman," she cried.

Mr. Mxyzptlk stopped laughing. "Careful, Miss Lane," he said. "Otherwise Superfish might do something to you!"

Lois's eyes grew wide with fear. Just then, the giant blowfish made a gurgling noise. It sounded like a human voice trying to say, "Look out!"

Sharp, orange spikes shot from the fish's body. They flew in all directions throughout the room. One of the spikes, as large as a spear, flew past Lois's feet. She jumped and threw herself behind a stone display table for protection.

Another spike stabbed through the museum director's skeleton and pinned him to the wall. More spikes broke statues and chandeliers and displays.

"You're making a mess, Superman," said the little imp. He flew down from the ceiling and snapped his fingers. Superman returned to his normal size and shape.

"I think you look better like that," said Mxy. "But what are we going to do about all this clutter? Hmmm."

Superman flew to Lois's side.

"Superman, what will we do?" asked Lois. "His magic is too powerful even for you."

"There's only one way to defeat that imp," whispered the Man of Steel. "If he says his name backwards, then he's banished back to the Fifth Dimension."

"How do we get him to say it?" said Lois.

"I have an idea," said Superman. "But I'll need your help."

CHAPTER 4

OCEAN CREATURES

"Oh, Superman!" called the wicked imp.

Superman raced over to Mr. Mxyzptlk. "Haven't you had enough fun, yet?" he asked the little man.

Mxy shook his head. "We have to clean up first," he said. "Didn't your mother ever tell you to pick up after you play?"

Lois looked over the edge of the stone table where she was hiding. What was Mxy planning next? Suddenly, her feet felt cold and wet.

Lois stared down at the marble floor. It was covered with an inch of warm water. "I have a bad feeling about this," she said.

Lois stood up and looked around the rest of the hall. Water was everywhere. The stairs to the second floor looked like a waterfall. In less than a minute, the water had reached her knees.

"Rub-a-dub-dub," said Mr. Mxyzptlk. "Time to clean!"

Superman stood in the middle of the hall, water swirling around his boots. "This has gone far enough," he said.

Mxy zigged and zagged through the air. "Don't even think of getting rid of this water, Super Duper Man," he said. "Because our poor fishy friends couldn't live without it."

The level of the water was now up to Superman's chest. He flew over to Lois and lifted her up. "We're getting out of here now," he said.

"Not so fast," said the little imp. "I put a special jinx on your museum. You and Miss Lane can't leave the building. Besides, it would be very rude of you to leave before my celebration is over!"

Still held in Superman's arms, Lois asked, "What's that sound?"

Superman stared at the marble walls of the exhibit hall. His powerful X-ray vision let him see through the stone. He saw large glass tanks in another room break and fall apart. The tanks had been holding the museum's other famous residents. Sharks!

Two enormous hammerhead sharks swam down the steps and into the exhibit hall. Superman flew toward the ceiling. He set Lois down on a stone ledge high above the water. "Wait here," he told her. Then he zoomed into the insect room. He found Jimmy floating in the water, holding onto a wooden pencil.

"I knew you'd show up," said the tiny teenager.

Superman held Jimmy gently in his hand and then soared back to Lois. "I have something for you," said the Man of Steel.

Superman dropped the teensy teenager in the woman's palm. "Don't tell me that's Jimmy!" she cried.

Jimmy held his hands to his ears. "Please, Miss Lane!" he said. "Not so loud."

"Hang on to the ledge," said Superman. "I've got to stop that imp somehow."

As he flew away, Lois called after him. "You have to find Clark Kent! He might be trapped in the museum!"

"I'll find him, Lois," said the super hero. "Don't worry."

The water rose higher and higher. More sea creatures were swimming below the sharks. Giant sea turtles and stingrays darted through the waves. Electric eels slithered and sparked.

The rushing water had been pressing against the windows of the museum. Now, several of the windows broke. The pressure was too strong. Water poured through the new openings like raging rivers, splashing onto the crowds outside.

"I'm not able to leave the museum to help those people," said Superman. "I can't break through Mxy's magic spell."

The Man of Steel flew back to the center of the hall. He stared up at the ceiling. The wires that had held the whale skeleton were still dangling free. Superman tied them together with super-speed and made one long wire. Then he made a loop and swung it out a broken window.

Like a superpowered cowboy, he lassoed the sharks and turtles and pulled them back inside the building. Then he used his heat-vision to repair the window glass and weld them shut.

"No fair," said Mr. Mxyzptlk. "I was trying to share my celebration with those silly people outside."

Then, the little imp snapped his fingers. "That's it!" he cried.

"Now what are you doing?" asked Superman.

RUMMMMMMMMBLE!

The Man of Steel stared out a window. He couldn't believe his eyes. The museum was rising into the air. Mr. Mxyzptlk had created gigantic crab legs on the bottom of the building. The stiff legs unfolded and lifted the entire museum off its foundation.

"The museum isn't a toy," Superman said. "You could seriously hurt someone."

"Don't be crabby," said Mxy. Then he chuckled. "Ha! I made a joke. Get it?"

Outside, men and women screamed. Taxis tried to rush away from the building but ran into other fleeing vehicles.

The huge museum monster began to march down the street. It scraped against other buildings on both sides of the street. Cement, metal, and broken glass rained down on the sidewalks.

"This show is going on the road," yelled Mxy happily. "If people can't visit the museum, then the museum will visit them. Isn't that a wonderful idea, Superman? Don't you think I'm generous?"

The little imp clapped his hands together and flew in a circle, round and round. Sparks flew out bchind him like fireworks. "This is the best party ever!" he said. "And I'm the perfect host!"

CHAPTER 5

THE WORST MONSTER

The museum monster marched through Metropolis on its giant crab legs. Buildings were smashed. Cars were crushed. People were injured. Mr. Mxyzptlk's selfish prank caused destruction throughout the city.

Superman stared out the museum window, unable to help. He knew he had to do something.

Suddenly, he turned and faced the floating imp. "This is your most amazing trick ever," he said.

Mxy's face lit up with delight. "You think so?" he cried. "You really, really think so?"

Superman nodded. "Only someone as clever and thoughtful as you, Mxy, could come up with this celebration," he said. "The people of Metropolis will never forget you. They'll talk about your museum party for years to come."

Bright tears glistened in the imp's eyes. "Oh, I'm so happy," he said.

"It's perfect," said Superman. "Except for —" Then he stopped.

"Except for what?" asked Mr. Mxyzptlk.

"Never mind," said Superman.

A worried frown covered the floating imp's face. "I want my party to be perfect," he wailed. "What else can I do, Superman?"

The Man of Steel stood for a moment in thought. "Well," he said slowly, "you want the people of Metropolis to enjoy the new exhibits at the museum, right?'

"Yes! Of course, I do," said Mr. Mxyzptlk.

"I'm just a little worried that some of the exhibits may scare them," said Superman.

"Scare them? Which ones?" Mxy asked.

Superman pointed up the marble stairs toward the upper floors. "We have an exhibit of dangerous animals," he said. "One of them is the creature that's most frightening to humans."

Mxy's eyes grew wide under his purple hat. "Really?" he asked in a whisper. "What is it called?"

"Humans don't even like the sound of its name," said Superman.

Superman leaned in closer. "Parents use the name to frighten bad children," he said. "But even grownups hate to hear it."

Mr. Mxyzptlk clapped his hands together. "I must see it," he cried. "If it is the world's worst monster, I must learn all about it. It would make a perfect pet!"

"Please, Mxy," said Superman in a serious tone. "Don't force people to see it. As I said, humans are terrified of the creature."

Mr. Mxyzptlk had an evil grin. "Oh, don't worry," he said. "I'll be very careful. You know how kind and caring I am."

Superman stared at the imp. "Very well," he said. "I'll show you the monster. Follow me." The Man of Steel flew up the marble stairs with the little man close behind him.

They soon arrived at another exhibit hall on the fourth floor. In the center of the room stood a tall, hairy stuffed animal. It had the body of a bear, the tusks of an elephant, the mane of a lion, and the long snout of an alligator. A long anteater's tongue dripped out of its jaws.

"It looks horrible." said Mr. Mxyzptlk.

"I told you," said Superman. "Now remember, don't even say the creature's name when you're around people. Humans hate the sound of it."

The little imp chuckled to himself. "They do, do they? Why, I'd never want to frighten people. Hmmmm."

Mr. Mxyzptlk moved closer to the terrible creature. He bent down and read the name of the creature on a metal sign.

Then Mr. Mxyzptlk read the sign aloud:

THE WORLD'S WORST MONSTER
Scientific Name: *Lktp Zyxm*

"Superman! You tricked me!" screamed the little imp. "You made me say my name backwards!"

Superman crossed his arms and smiled. "Good-bye, Mxy. Enjoy the Fifth Dimension."

The little man began to fade. His purple hat and tiny boots were just dark smudges on the air. "There is no creature like that, is there, Superman?" he asked.

"Of course, not, Mxy. I made it up," said the Man of Steel. "I used parts of different animals on display throughout the museum. With my super-speed, I took the parts and made this fake animal. I moved so fast you never even saw me do it."

"AAAAAAAAhhhhhhhhhhh!" With a loud **POP!** the little imp disappeared.

Superman flew downstairs to rescue Lois and Jimmy from the ledge near the ceiling. As he did, a strange thing happened. The museum's crab legs vanished. The whale skeleton was hanging back on its wires. Jimmy was his regular size. The museum director was no longer just a walking skeleton. The crowds outside acted like nothing had happened that morning.

"Is it all over?" asked Lois.

"When Mr. Mxyzptlk returned to his home dimension, all his magic disappeared with him," said Superman.

Jimmy Olsen gazed out a window. "Wow," he said. "The museum is back in its regular place. It's like it never even moved."

The museum director rushed up to Superman and shook his hand. "Thank you, Superman. I owe you my life," he said. "And if you'll please excuse me," he added, looking at his watch, "I need to let in our visitors."

He raced away to the front doors.

Suddenly, Lois looked worried. "I forgot about Clark," she said. "He was somewhere in the building. Oh, Jimmy, you don't think he drowned, do you?"

"Don't worry, Lois," said Superman. "He's just fine. I saw him rush outside looking for the police earlier. Luckily, he never got trapped inside with the rest of us."

"But now he's caught in that crowd," said Jimmy. "Poor Mr. Kent."

Lois simply shook her head. "Clark Kent always seems to miss the action," she said. Then she turned to look at the Man of Steel. "It's a good thing you never do, Superman."

But the super hero had already flown away.

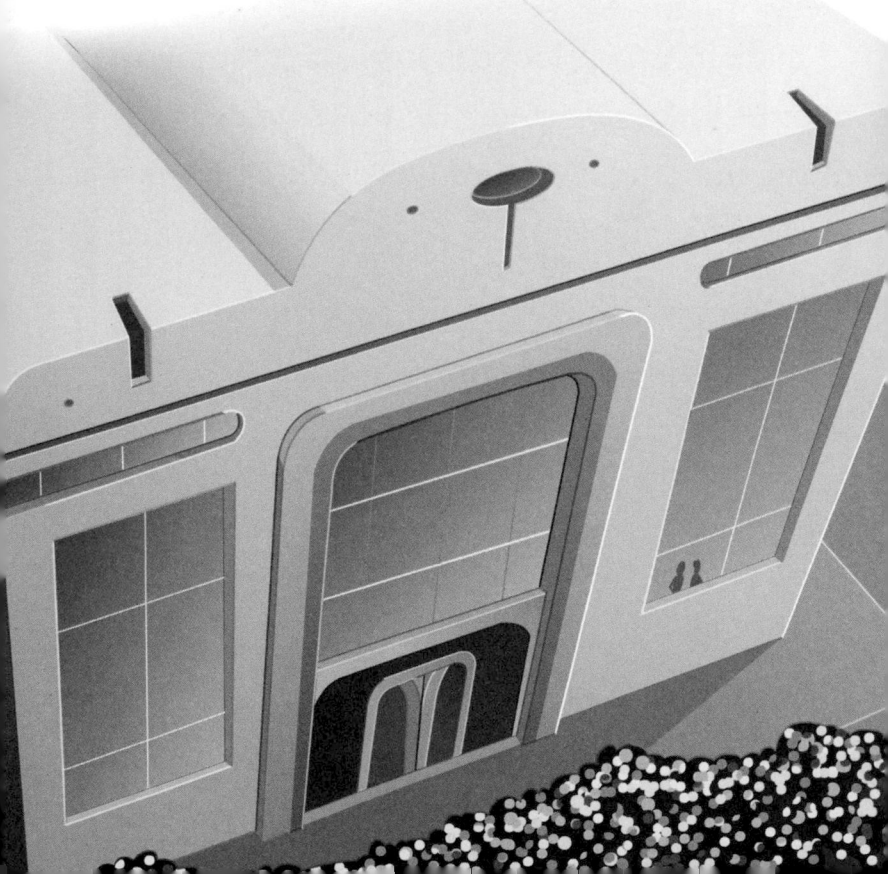

WHO IS MXY?

Mr. Mxyzptlk, or Mxy for short, is a mischievous imp from the Fifth Dimension. In this wacky world, everyone has strange magical powers. Unfortunately, Mxy likes using his terrible tricks to torment his greatest foe. Every 90 days, he travels to Earth and tries to humiliate Superman with his pathetic pranks. Fortunately, the Man of Steel knows exactly how to get rid of the puny pest . . . at least for a while.

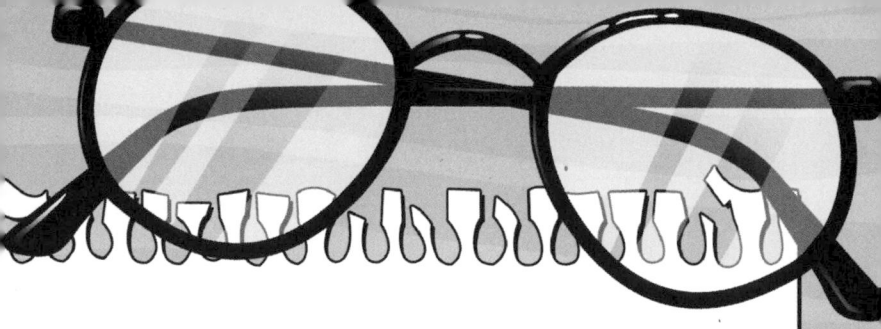

- To send Mr. Mxyzptlk back to the Fifth Dimension, Superman must trick the miniature magician into saying or writing his name backwards.

- Mr. Mxyzptlk's strange name is pronounced "Mix-yez-pittle-ick."

- Only a few people know that Clark Kent is really the Man of Steel. Mxy is one of them.

- Superman also has some weaknesses. The Man of Steel cannot defend himself against magic. He's often helpless against the tiny trickster's spells.

BIOGRAPHIES

Michael Dahl is the author of more than 200 books for children and young adults. He has won the AEP Distinguished Achievement Award three times for his non-fiction.
His Finnegan Zwake mystery series was shortlisted twice by the Anthony and Agatha awards. He has also written the Library of Doom series and the Dragonblood books. He is a featured speaker at conferences around the country on graphic novels and high-interest books for boys.

Dan Schoening was born in Victoria, B.C. Canada. From an early age, Dan has had a passion for animation and comic books. Currently, Dan does freelance work in the animation and game industry and spends a lot of time with his lovely little daughter, Paige.

GLOSSARY

banished (BAN-ishd)—sent someone away from a place without the possibility of return

chandelier (shan-duh-LEER)—a light fixture that hangs from the ceiling

disguise (diss-GIZE)—to dress in a way that hides your identity

exoskeleton (eks-oh-SKEL-uht-uhn)—a bony structure on the outside of an animal, like the shell of a crab or lobster

glistened (GLISS-uhnd)—shined in a sparkling way

imp (IMP)—a sly or evil little creature

impostor (im-POSS-tor)—someone who pretends to be something that he or she is not

mischievous (MISS-chuh-vuhss)—playful behavior that is annoying or harmful to others

supersonic (soo-pur-SON-ik)—faster than the speed of sound

DISCUSSION QUESTIONS

1. Superman cannot defend himself against Mxy's magic with super-strength. What abilities does Superman use to stop the tiny trickster?

2. Clark Kent is secretly Superman. Why do you think he keeps his identity a secret? If you were a super hero, would you tell anyone?

3. Many books are written and illustrated by two different people. Would you rather be an author or an illustrator? Why?

WRITING PROMPTS

1. If Mxy says his name backwards, he is sent back to the Fifth Dimension. Rearrange the letters in your own name. How many different words can you make?

2. Mxy returns to Earth every 90 days. What tricks do you think he'll play next time? How will Superman get rid of him?

3. Even the Man of Steel has weaknesses. He cannot defend himself against magic. List some of your own weaknesses, and then list some of your strengths.

MORE NEW
SUPERMAN
ADVENTURES!

THE MENACE OF METALLO

LAST SON OF KRYPTON

THE STOLEN SUPERPOWERS

TOYS OF TERROR

UNDER THE RED SUN

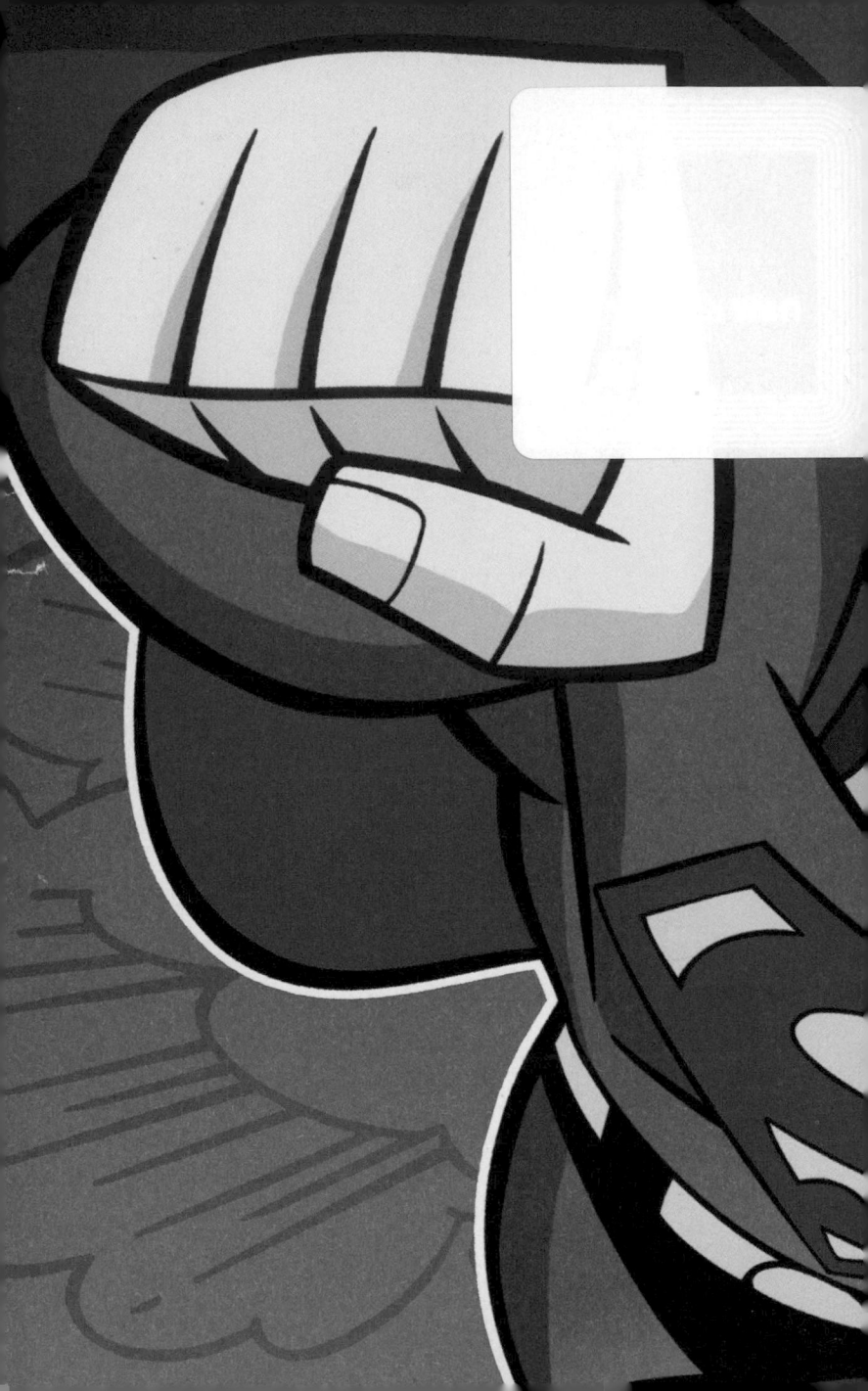